我们还会再见吗

Parting

苗勇刚　贾宇萍　编译

中国出版集团　现代出版社

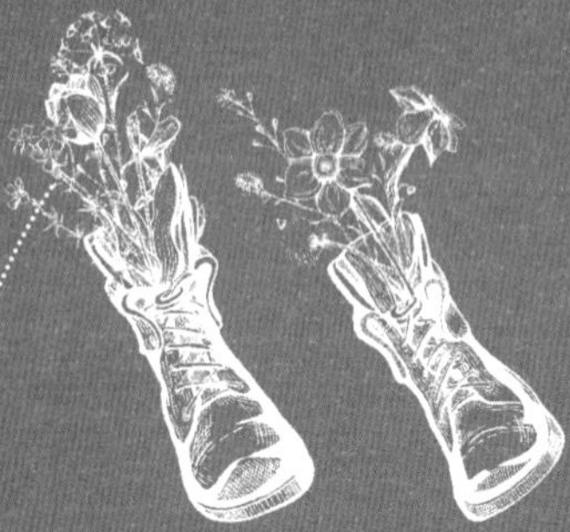

contents

目录

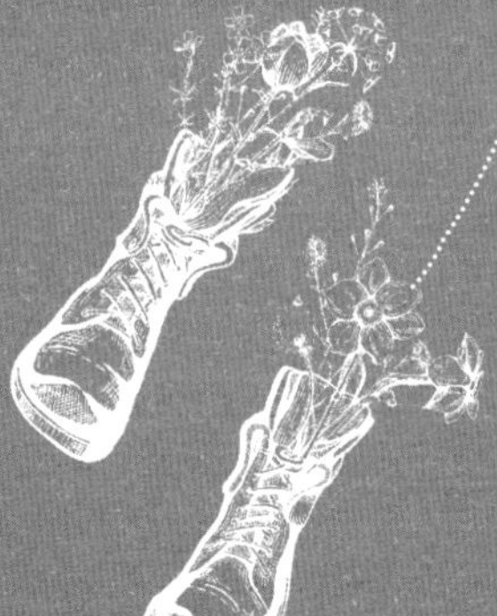

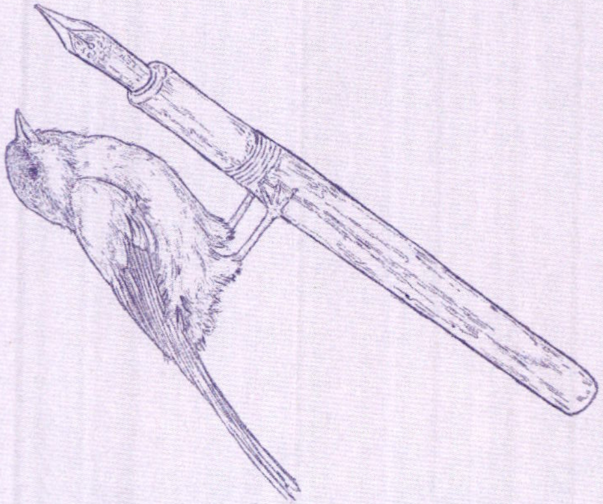

Bidding Farewell

生离

No. 1

And Will You Leave Me Thus?

Thomas Wyatt

And will you leave me thus?
Say nay, say nay, for shame,
To save you from blame,
Of all my grief and grame.
And will you leave me thus?
Say no, say no!

Will you leave me thus,
that has loved you so long,
In wealth and woe among?
And is your heart so strong
As for to leave me thus?
Say no, say no!

No. 1

你就这样离我而去?

托马斯·怀亚特

难道你就这样离我而去?
说不吧！说不！多么可耻！
免得因我所有的悲惨
让你遭受诸多的责难。
难道你就这样离我而去?
说不吧，说不！

难道你就这样离我而去?
我曾爱你那么久长，
无论富裕悲愁时光
你的心怎可如此刚强，
忍心就这样离我而去?
说不吧，说不！

And will you leave me thus,
That has given you my heart,
Never for to depart,
Neither for pain nor smart;
And will you leave me thus?
Say no, say no!

And will you leave me thus,
And have no more pity
Of him that loves you?
Alas, your cruelty!
And will you leave me thus?
Say no, say no!

难道你就这样离我而去?
我的心早已奉献给你,
无论何种痛苦悲戚
永远不能把你背弃;
难道你就这样离我而去?
说不吧,说不!

难道你就这样离我而去?
对那个深爱你的人
心中没有半丝怜悯?
啊呀,你好残忍!
难道你就这样离我而去?
说不吧,说不!

托马斯·怀亚特爵士

1503—1542,英国诗人、政治家,开创英国十四行诗体。著名诗歌有《他们躲着我》《我的诗琴,醒来吧》《在永恒中》等。

No. 2

Departure

Arthur Rimbaud

Everything seen...

The vision gleams in every air.

Everything had...

The far sound of cities, in the evening,

In sunlight, and always.

Everything known...

O Tumult! O Visions! These are the stops of life.

Departure

in affection, and shining sounds.

No. 2

离去

阿尔蒂尔·兰波[ଓ]

曾看到的一切……
每处空气中闪烁的幻景
曾拥有的一切……
城市传来的喧嚣之声，
在夜晚，在日间，始终如一。
曾明悉的一切……
那喧闹！那幻景！都是生命的驿站。

离去，
伴着爱，和闪光的声响。

ଓ 让·尼古拉·阿尔蒂尔·兰波

1854—1891，19世纪法国著名诗人，早期象征主义诗歌的代表人物，超现实主义诗歌的鼻祖，代表作品《醉舟》《地狱一季》《彩画集》等。

No. 3

Why the Roses Are So Pale?

Heinrich Heine

Dearest, canst thou tell me why
The rose should be so pale?
And why the azure violet
Should wither in the vale?
And why the lark should in the cloud
So sorrowfully sing?
And why from loveliest balsam-buds
A scent of death should spring?

No. 3

为什么玫瑰如此苍白？

海因里希·海涅

最亲爱的人啊， 你能否告诉我
玫瑰为何憔悴？
为什么天青的紫罗兰
会在山谷里枯萎？
为何百灵鸟在云端
唱着椎心泣血的歌曲？
为什么最可爱的香脂芽，
会散发出死亡的气息？

And why the sun upon the mead
So chillingly should frown?
And why the earth should, like a grave,
Be moldering and brown?
And why it is that I myself
So languishing should be?
And why it is, my heart of hearts,
That thou forsake me?

草地上的阳光
何以如此冷酷地蹙眉？
那棕褐的大地，
何以像坟墓般地发霉？
为什么是我自己
变得破碎支离？
我的心肝儿啊，究竟为什么，
为什么你要将我抛弃？

☙ 海因里希·海涅

1797—1856，德国著名抒情诗人和散文家，代表作品有《罗曼采罗》《佛罗伦萨之夜》《哈尔茨山游记》《德国，一个冬天的童话》等。

No. 4

A Valediction Forbidding Mourning

John Donne

As virtuous men pass mildly away,
And whisper to their souls to go,
Whilst some of their sad friends do say,
"Now his breath goes," and some say, "No."

So let us melt, and make no noise,
No tear—floods, nor sigh—tempests move ;
'Twere profanation of our joys
To tell the laity our love.

Moving of th' earth brings harms and fears ;
Men reckon what it did, and meant ;

No. 4

别离辞：莫悲哀

约翰·多恩

正如德高之人安然离世，
对灵魂轻轻地说一声走，
悲伤的朋友们有些会说，
“他去了”，有的说“没有”。

我们平和些，不要作声，
莫挥泪如潮，叹气如雨；
要对俗人讲我们的爱情
那是在亵渎我们的欢愉。

地震会带来灾害和恐慌，
人们会猜它究竟要怎样

But trepidation of the spheres,
 Though greater far, is innocent.
Dull sublunary lovers' love
—Whose soul is sense—cannot admit
Of absence, 'cause it doth remove
The thing which elemented it.

But we by a love so much refined,
 That ourselves know not what it is,
Inter—assurèd of the mind,
Care less, eyes, lips and hands to miss.

Our two souls therefore, which are one,
Though I must go, endure not yet
A breach, but an expansion,
 Like gold to aery thinness beat.

If they be two, they are two so
As stiff twin compasses are two ;

可是那宇宙天体的震动，
虽然大得多，却总无妨。
世俗男女彼此相好，
（他们只关注感官）就最忌
别离，因为那就会取消
组成爱恋的那一套东西。

但我们的爱情精纯洁净，
自己都不知道是何念头
相互在心灵上得到保证，
不在乎触碰眼睛、嘴、手。

我俩的灵魂打成了一片，
虽说我得走，却并不能
破裂，而只是向外伸延，
像金子打到薄薄的一层。

即便是两个，却也这样
和一副圆规的情况相同；

Thy soul, the fix'd foot, makes no show
To move, but doth, if th' other do.

And though it in the centre sit,
Yet, when the other far doth roam,
It leans, and hearkens after it,
And grows erect, as that comes home.

Such wilt thou be to me, who must,
Like th' other foot, obliquely run ;
Thy firmness makes my circle just,
And makes me end where I begun.

你的灵魂是不动的定脚，
但另一脚一移它也会动。

虽然它一直是坐在中央，
可当另一个去远方游历，
它会侧过身，追随四方；
那个一回家，它就直起。

你对我就要这样，我会
像那只动脚，侧身打转；
你的坚定让我准确移位，
终结在最初开始的地方。

约翰·多恩

1572—1631，英国诗人，代表作品有《日出》《歌谣与十四行诗》《给圣父的赞美诗》。

No. 5

Sorrow of Separation

Rabindranath Tagore

It is the pang of separation that spreads throughout
The world and gives birth to shapes innumerable in the infinite sky.
It is this sorrow of separation that gazes
In silence all nights from star to star
And becomes lyric among rustling leaves
In rainy darkness of July.

It is this overspreading pain that
Deepens into loves and desires,
Into sufferings and joy in human homes;
And this it is that ever melts and
Flows in songs through my poet's heart.

No. 5

离殇

泰戈尔 ꧁

离别的痛苦蔓延在整个世间，
在无尽的天空中产生了无穷的形象。
整夜默望着天空繁星的
正是这离殇
在七月的阴雨中化作情诗，
在萧萧枝叶间飘荡。

正是这弥漫的伤痛
深化成爱和欲望，
升华为人间的痛苦与欢畅；
也正是它，在我诗人的心中
融化成曲 倏然流淌。

꧁ 拉宾德拉纳特·泰戈尔

1861—1941，印度诗人、文学家、社会活动家、哲学家和印度民族主义者。代表作有《吉檀迦利》《飞鸟集》《眼中沙》《四个人》《家庭与世界》《园丁集》《新月集》《最后的诗篇》《戈拉》《文明的危机》等。

No. 6

To Lucasta, Going to the Wars

Richard Lovelace

Tell me not, sweet, I am unkind,
That from the nunnery
Of thy chaste breast and quiet mind
To war and arms I fly.
True, a new mistress now I chase,
The first foe in the field;
And with a stronger faith embrace
A sword, a horse, a shield.
Yet this inconstancy is such
As you too shall adore;
could not love thee, dear, so much,
Loved I not honour more.

No. 6

出征前致露卡斯塔

理查德·勒夫莱斯

爱人，莫责我无情义，
离开你圣洁的胸房，
抛下你的温柔和静谧，
奔向那武器和疆场。
是的，我要另结新欢，
寻找战场第一个敌人，
拥抱战马盾牌和刀剑
以我坚定赤诚的心。
然而，这种三心二意
你也定会倾慕于此，
若我不如此醉心荣耀，
便也不会如此爱你。

理查德·勒夫莱斯

1617—1657，英国17世纪“骑士派”诗人，代表作有《狱中致爱尔西娅》《出征前致露卡斯塔》等。

No. 7

So We'll Go No More a Roving

George Gordon Byron

So, we'll go no more a roving
So late into the night,
Though the heart be still as loving,
And the moon be still as bright.
For the sword outwears its sheath,
And the soul wears out the breast,
And the heart must pause to breathe,
And love itself have rest.
Though the night was made for loving,
And the day returns too soon,
Yet we'll go no more a roving
By the light of the moon.

No. 7

那我们不再一起漫步

乔治·戈登·拜伦

那我们不再一起漫步，
消磨这幽静的夜晚，
尽管这颗心仍旧爱着，
尽管月光依然灿烂。
因为利剑会磨破剑鞘，
胸怀也因灵魂疲惫，
躁动的心儿需要喘息，
狂热的爱也需小憩。
尽管夜适合倾吐爱意
天光很快就要放亮，
但我们不再一起漫步，
踏着这灿烂的月光。

乔治·戈登·拜伦

1788—1824，英国19世纪初期伟大的浪漫主义诗人，代表作有《恰尔德·哈洛尔德游记》《唐璜》等。

No. 8

Departure

by Sylvia Plath

The figs on the fig tree in the yard are green;
Green, also, the grapes on the green vine
Shading the bricked porch tiles.
The money's run out.

How nature, sensing this, compounds her bitters.
Ungifted, ungrieved, our leavetaking.
The sun shines on unripe corn.
Cats play in the stalks.

Retrospect shall not often such penury—
Sun's brass, the moon's steely patinas,

No. 8

离别

西尔维娅·普拉斯[08]

院里树上的无花果是绿色；
碧绿藤蔓上的葡萄也是绿色。
藤遮住了门廊上砖红的瓦片。
钱已经花完。

感知这一切，自然会怎样缓解痛苦。
我们的分手，无能为力，无动于衷。
阳光依旧在未成熟的玉米上闪耀，
猫儿仍然嬉闹在秸秆中。

回忆不该如此匮乏——
太阳的明媚，月色的皎洁，

The leaden slag of the world—

But always expose

The scraggy rock spit shielding the town's blue bay

Against which the brunt of outer sea

Beats, is brutal endlessly.

Gull—fouled, a stone hut

Bares its low lintel to corroding weathers:

Across the jut of ochreous rock

Goats shamble, morose, rank—haired,

To lick the sea—salt.

世界灰暗的熔渣
总是显露着
嶙峋的怪石，护卫小镇碧蓝的海湾
免受外海的侵袭，
海浪的拍击是永不停息的残暴。
石洞中，海鸥拥挤，

低小的门楣暴露在腐蚀的天气，
一只忧郁的脏山羊步履蹒跚
越过褐红岩石的凸起，
只为了舔舐海盐。

☙ 西尔维娅·普拉斯

1932—1963，美国自白派诗人的代表，代表作有《巨人及其他诗歌》等。

No. 9

On Monsieur's Departure

Elizabeth I

I grieve and dare not show my discontent,
I love and yet am forced to seem to hate,
I do, yet dare not say I ever meant,
I seem stark mute but inwardly do prate.

I am and not, I freeze and yet am burned,
Since from myself another self I turned.
My care is like my shadow in the sun,
Follows me flying, flies when pursue it,
Stands and lies by me, doth what I have done.

No. 9

先生离别之际

伊丽莎白一世

我满怀忧伤，却不敢表露不平，
我满腔热爱，却只能强装讨厌，
我如此行径，却难表真实心情，
口中缄默无言，心中万语千言。

煎熬是非之间，辗转冰火之中，
只因为我已将自己分成了两半。
我的关心，宛如太阳下的阴影，
翩翩随我身形，寻它却是不见，
时刻立卧身侧，做我所做一切。

His too familiar care doth make me rue it.
No means I find to rid him from my breast,
Till by the end of things it be suppressed.
Some gentler passion slide into my mind,
For I am soft and made of melting snow;

Or be more cruel, Love, and so be kind.
Let me or float or sink, be high or low.
Or let me live with some more sweet content,
Or die and so forget what love are meant.

他熟稔的关心总让我心怀懊悔，
因为我无法将他驱出我的世界，
直到末世来临，此情方可平息。
一些甜蜜爱意溜进了我的脑袋，
因我天性温和，宛如冰水造就；

爱神，残忍些，或者慈悲为怀。
让我飞升天堂，或是直堕地狱。
要让我活，就多赐些爱的甜蜜，
要么让我死去，忘却爱的意义。

伊丽莎白一世

1533—1603，英国都铎王朝最后一位君主，其统治时期被称作英国历史上的“黄金时代”。

No. 10

A Red, Red Rose

Robert Burns

O my Luve is like a red, red rose
That's newly sprung in June;
O my Luve is like the melody
That's sweetly played in tune.

So fair art thou, my bonnie lass,
So deep in luve am I;
And I will luve thee still, my dear,
Till a' the seas gang dry.

No. 10

一朵红红的玫瑰

罗伯特·彭斯

啊　我的爱人像一朵红红的玫瑰
六月刚刚绽放；
啊　我的爱人像一首美妙的乐曲
音调甜美清扬。

你是如此漂亮，我美丽的姑娘，
我把你深深爱恋；
我会永远爱你，我心爱的姑娘，
直到四海枯干。

Till a' the seas gang dry, my dear,
And the rocks melt wi' the sun;
I will love thee still, my dear,
While the sands o' life shall run.

And fare thee weel, my only luve!
And fare thee weel awhile!
And I will come again, my luve,
Though it were ten thousand mile.

直到四海枯干，我亲爱的，
太阳熔化石块；
我会永远爱你，我亲爱的，
只要生命尚在。

再见了，我唯一的爱！
我们要暂时分离！
我一定会回来，我的爱人
哪怕相隔万里。

罗伯特·彭斯

1759—1796，苏格兰农民诗人，在英国文学史上占有特殊重要的地位。他复活并丰富了苏格兰民歌，代表作有《友谊地久天长》《两只狗》《一朵红红的玫瑰》《往昔的时光》等。

No.11

After Parting

Sara Teasdale

Oh I have sown my love so wide
That he will find it everywhere;
It will awake him in the night,
It will enfold him in the air.

I set my shadow in his sight
And I have winged it with desire,
That it may be a cloud by day
And in the night a shaft of fire.

No. 11

离别之后

莎拉·蒂斯黛尔[ω]

我把爱如此广阔地播撒，
将陪伴无处不在地奉送。
爱替我在暗夜将他唤醒，
爱代我在风中与他相拥。

我派我的影子与他随行，
并以渴望装备它的翅膀。
好让它在日间化为云朵，
在黑夜里变成闪闪火光。

ω 莎拉·蒂斯黛尔

1884—1933，美国现代抒情诗人，1918 年美国诗协会年度诗人奖和哥伦比亚大学诗协会奖的获得者。

No. 12

First Farewell to J.G.

Ephelia

Farewell my dearer half, joy of my heart,
Heaven only knows how loth I am to part:
Whole Months but hours seem, when you are here,
When absent, every Minute is a Year:

Might I but always see thy charming Face,
I'de live on Racks, and wish no easier place.
But we must part, your Interest says we must;
Fate, me no longer with such Treasure trust.

No. 12

向 J.G. 首次告别

埃菲利亚

再见，我的爱，我的另一半，
天知道与你分开我多不情愿。
你在我身边时，如白驹过隙，
不在我身边时，却度秒如年。

希望能永远见到你迷人面容，
真想变成行李可以随你远行。
但是为了前途我们终将分手，
命运不再让我拥有这块珍宝。

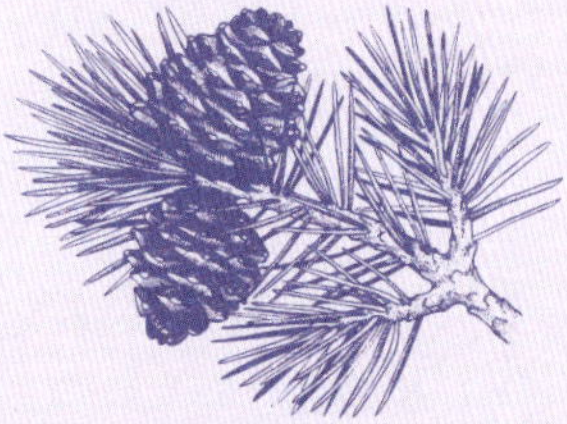

I wou'd not tax you with Inconstancy,
Yet Strephon, you are not so kind as I:
No Interest, no nor Fate it self has pow'r
To tempt me from the Idol I adore:
But since you needs will go, may Africk be
Kinder to you, than Europe is to me:

May all you meet and every thing you view
Give you such Transport as I met in you.
May no sad thoughts disturb your quiet mind,
Except you'l think of her you left behind.

我断不会追究你的有始无终，
但是相思之苦却是那么煎熬。
哪怕命运也未拥有如此力量，
诱惑我离开我所热爱的偶像。
既然你一定要走，祝愿非洲
对你比欧洲对我要更加友善。

愿你所遇的人，所见的事物，
都能赐给你你曾予我的欣欢。
愿忧伤莫把你平静心情践踏，
除非回忆到你曾经抛下的她。

埃菲利亚

是玛丽维利尔夫人、列治文和伦诺克斯公爵夫人的笔名，国王查尔斯一世的养女，英国17世纪女诗人。

No. 13

Farewell

Anne Brontë

Farewell to thee! but not farewell
To all my fondest thoughts of thee:
Within my heart they still shall dwell;
And they shall cheer and comfort me.
O, beautiful, and full of grace!
If thou hadst never met mine eye,
I had not dreamed a living face
Could fancied charms so far outvie.

If I may ne'er behold again
That form and face so dear to me,

No. 13

惜别

安妮·勃朗特

与你告别，但却难以抹去
我珍藏的对你最美的记忆。
在我心中，它们仍将存续
它们给我鼓舞，予我慰藉。
哦，如此美丽，如此优雅！
如果你从未进入我的视线，
我从未梦见这鲜活的面颊
竟然超过一切想象的容颜。

如果，我再没有机会见到
那如此可爱的面庞与形体，

Nor hear thy voice, still would I fain
Preserve, for aye, their memory.
That voice, the magic of whose tone
Can wake an echo in my breast,
Creating feelings that, alone,
Can make my tranced spirit blest.

That laughing eye, whose sunny beam
My memory would not cherish less; —
And oh, that smile! whose joyous gleam
Nor mortal language can express.

Adieu, but let me cherish, still,
The hope with which I cannot part.
Contempt may wound, and coldness chill,
But still it lingers in my heart.
And who can tell but Heaven, at last,
May answer all my thousand prayers,
And bid the future pay the past
With joy for anguish, smiles for tears?

再也听不到你声音的美妙，
我会欣然，留存这些记忆。
那声音，是谁音调的魔力
唤起我心怀里激荡的回声，
让我感情迸发喷薄，独自
将沉睡的灵魂从梦中唤醒。

那笑意盈眸，如阳光闪耀
我将刻骨不忘，永铭于心；
那盎然欢颜！如快乐普照
又岂是人间凡语能够述陈。

再见了，但我将依然珍存
我始终难以割舍的这希望。
冷漠可刺骨，轻蔑能伤人，
但这记忆仍萦绕我的心房。
但谁会知道，或许是上苍，
最终他将回应我所有祈求，
诏令未来对过去做出补偿
喜悦代离殇，欢笑代泪流？

安妮·勃朗特

1820—1849，19世纪英国小说家、诗人，代表作品有小说《艾格尼斯·格雷》《怀尔德菲尔府的房客》。

No. 14

Farewell

Rabindranath Tagore

I have got my leave. Bid me farewell, my brothers!
I bow to you all and take my departure.
Here I give back the keys of my door
and I give up all claims to my house.
I only ask for last kind words from you.
We were neighbors for long,
but I received more than I could give.
Now the day has dawned
and the lamp that lit my dark corner is out.
A summons has come and I am ready for my journey.

No. 14

告别

泰戈尔

我将远行，再见了，兄弟们！
我恭别你们，踏上离别路。
我归还了家门的钥匙，
放弃对房子的所有权利，
只求你最后的道别。
我们为邻已久，
但我得到的比我给予的要多。
天色已亮，
点亮我黑暗角落的灯已经熄灭。
召唤已经到来，我就要启程。

No. 15

On Leaving Some Friends at an Early Hour

John Keats

Give me a golden pen, and let me lean
On heap'd up flowers, in regions clear, and far;
Bring me a tablet whiter than a star,
Or hand of hymning angel, when 'tis seen
The silver strings of heavenly harp atween:

And let there glide by many a pearly car,
Pink robes, and wavy hair, and diamond jar,
And half discovered wings, and glances keen.

No. 15

清晨别友人有感

约翰·济慈

给我一支金笔吧，让我靠守
一簇花，在某地，明媚遥远；
给我一块比星星更白的石板
或者，唱着圣歌的天使的手
正在神圣竖琴的银弦间弹奏。

让珍珠的车驾，粉红的衣衫，
波浪似的卷鬓发，钻石的花坛，
半张翅翼和锐利的眼神飘走。

The while let music wander round my ears,
And as it reaches each delicious ending,
Let me write down a line of glorious tone,
And full of many wonders of the spheres:
For what a height my spirit is contending!
'Tis not content so soon to be alone.

让那音乐在我耳边萦绕不去，
直到每一首曲子甜美地告终，
就让我写下一行辉煌的曲调
让它能讲述天庭的百般奇趣：
啊，我的心正在向高峰攀登！
它不甘心这样快地孤独寂寥。

约翰·济慈

1795—1821，英国浪漫主义诗人，
代表诗作有《夜莺颂》《希腊古瓮颂》
《秋颂》《忧郁颂》等。

No. 16

Departure

Johann Wolfgang von Goethe

With many a thousand kiss not yet content,
At length with One kiss I was forced to go;
After that bitter parting's depth of woe,
I deem'd the shore from which my steps I bent,
Its hills, streams, dwellings, mountains, as I went,
A pledge of joy, till daylight ceased to glow;
Then on my sight did blissful visions grow
In the dim—lighted, distant firmament,
And when at length the sea confined my gaze,
My ardent longing fill'd my heart once more;
What I had lost, unwillingly I sought.
Then Heaven appear'd to shed its kindly rays:
Methought that all I had possess'd of yore
Remain'd still mine that I was reft of nought.

No. 16

离去

约翰·沃尔夫冈·冯·歌德

几千个吻也不能让我心甘，
最后一吻过去我不得不走，
苦涩离别深切的痛苦之后，
我认定我不愿离别的海岸、
途经的溪水、居所和高山，
都是欢乐，直到天色黑透；
然后幸福幻景闪过我眼眸，
在那黯淡而且遥远的天边，
最终大海阻止了我的凝望，
心田再次充满热切的渴求；
我曾失去的，不愿再寻觅。
但天空洒下它仁慈的光芒：
我认识到，过去我的拥有
依然属于我，我一无所失。

约翰·沃尔夫冈·冯·歌德

1749—1832，德国著名思想家、作家、科学家，魏玛的古典主义最著名的代表，代表作品有《少年维特之烦恼》《浮士德》等。

No. 17

Departure

Henry Van Dyke

Oh, why are you shining so bright, big Sun,
And why is the garden so gay?
Do you know that my days of delight are done,
Do you know I am going away?
If you covered your face with a cloud, I 'd dream
You were sorry for me in my pain,
And the heads of the flowers all bowed would seem
To be weeping with me in the rain.

No. 17

离开

亨利·范·戴克

啊，太阳，你为何如此闪亮？
花园又为何如此欢快？
你可知我的幸福时光已终场，
你可知，我就要离开？
如果你以云遮面，我会猜想
你是为我的痛苦惋惜，
花园的花儿都低下头，好像
在雨中与我一同哭泣。

But why is your head so low, sweet heart,
And why are your eyes overcast?
Are they clouded because you know we must part,
Do you think this embrace is our last?
Then kiss me again, and again, and again,
Look up as you bid me good-bye!
For your face is too dear for the stain of a tear,
And your smile is the sun in my sky.

但亲爱的，你为什么低着头？
为了阴霾遮蔽了眼睛？
难道因为你知道我们要分手，
以为这是最后的拥吻？
那就再吻我吧，再多吻几次，
抬起头，跟我说再见！
你可爱的面容怎可沾染泪滴，
你若微笑，便是晴天。

亨利·范·戴克

1852—1933，美国作家、教育家，代表作品有短篇小说《别的聪明人》《第一棵圣诞树》等。

No. 18

We Never Said Farewell

Mary Elizabeth Coleridge

We never said farewell,
nor even looked Our last upon each other,
for no sign was made when we the linkèd chain unhooked
And broke the level line.

And here we dwell together, side by side,
Our places fixed for life upon the chart.
Two islands that the roaring seas divide
Are not more far apart.

No. 18

我们从不说再见

玛丽·伊丽莎白·柯勒律治

我们从不说再见，
也不会再彼此看最后一眼，
只因我们打破平静生活的分离
未留下任何印痕。

我们在这里栖居，紧挨着，
人生位置早已经刻入图版。
两个岛被咆哮的大海分隔，
不会再变得更远。

玛丽·伊丽莎白·柯勒律治

1861—1907，英国诗人、小说家，代表作品有小说《双面国王》、诗歌《蓝鸟》等。

No. 19

Farewell

Johann Wolfgang von Goethe

To break one's word is pleasure—fraught,
To do one's duty gives a smart;
While man, alas! will promise nought,
That is repugnant to his heart.

Using some magic strains of yore,
Thou lurest him, when scarcely calm,
On to sweet folly's fragile bark once more,
Renewing, doubling chance of harm.

No. 19

再见

约翰·沃尔夫冈·冯·歌德

打破誓言充满了喜悦，
尽职尽责多令人痛苦；
人啊，却总不喜承诺，
那东西啊，心也厌恶。

借助古老魔法的束缚，
你引诱他，却难平静，
披上甜美愚蠢的衣服，
那会产生双倍的伤痛。

Why seek to hide thyself from me?
Fly not my sight—be open then!
Known late or early it must be,
And here thou hast thy word again.

My duty is fulfill'd to-day,
No longer will I guard thee from surprise;
But, oh, forgive the friend who from thee turns away,
And to himself for refuge flies!

你为何非要把我逃避？
莫离视野，敞开心田！
你知道早晚定会如此，
这里你才能再次发言。

我的责任今日已结束，
再不会让你免于意外；
原谅离你而去的朋友，
正逃向自己寻求依赖。

No. 20

Farewell to Eliza

Robert Burns

FROM thee, Eliza, I must go,
And from my native shore;
The cruel fates between us throw
A boundless ocean's roar:

But boundless oceans, roaring wide,
Between my love and me,
They never, never can divide
My heart and soul from thee.

No. 20

与伊莱扎告别

罗伯特·彭斯

伊莱扎，我要说再见，
从我家乡的海岸离开，
残酷命运在我们中间
抛下一片咆哮的大海。

尽管这无边际的大海
咆哮着分开我和爱人，
却永远无法从你身上
分隔出我的心与灵魂。

Farewell, farewell, Eliza dear,
The maid that I adore!
A boding voice is in mine ear,
We part to meet no more!

But the latest throb that leaves my heart,
While Death stands victor by,
That throb, Eliza, is thy part,
And thine that latest sigh!

再见，亲爱的伊莱扎，
我全心全意把你眷恋！
耳边却想起不详的话，
这次别离，无缘再见！

但是我心最后的悸动，
会是死神在身边伫立，
那悸动是因忆起了你，
你才是我最后的叹息！

Music, When Soft Voices Die 当轻柔之音消逝，音乐 Away Now You Depart From Me 如今你已经离我而去 A Farewell 告别 A Farewell 告别 Break, Break, Break 破碎，破碎，破碎 Remember 记 The Last Night that She Lived 最后一夜 A Dirge 挽歌 The Last Waltz 最后的华尔兹 Song 歌 A Dream Within a Dream 梦中之梦 Stanzas. —April, 1814 诗节——1814 年 4 月 Regret for the Departure of Friends 为朋友的离去感叹 The Last Farewell 最后的告别

Parting Forever

处别

No. 1

Music, When Soft Voices Die

Percy Bysshe Shelley

Music, when soft voices die,
Vibrates in the memory;
Odours, when sweet violets sicken,
Live within the sense they quicken.

Rose leaves, when the rose is dead,
Are heap'd for the belovèd's bed;
And so thy thoughts, when thou art gone,
Love itself shall slumber on.

No. 1

当轻柔之音消逝，音乐

珀西·比希·雪莱

当轻柔的声音消逝，音乐
却还在记忆中震颤；
当甜美的紫罗兰枯萎，芬芳
还在生机中绵延。

当玫瑰凋零时，花叶
撒落成情人的床帏；
因此，当你离去时，你的思想
将成为爱情的衾被。

珀西·比希·雪莱

1792—1822，英国浪漫主义诗人，代表作有《西风颂》《解放了的普罗米修斯》等。

No. 2

Away Now You Depart From Me

Moses Ocharo

Away now you depart from me
And mount the chariot heaven bound
You fleet in sleep, without a sound
Gone forever, left me only your memory
And I know my tears hath in vain
As you hath both deaf and mute
Left me hanging in half salute
To lull my heart that tears drain
But at last you can now rest
In peace, and forget all your sorrows
Without a worry of todays and tomorrows
Only rejoice with your family in jest
Still i say your stay was too brief
And still i do suspend my disbelief.

No. 2

如今你已经离我而去

摩西·奥沙罗 ♂

如今你已经离我而去，
登上马车，前往天堂，
在梦中飞驰没有声响，
一去不归，徒留追忆。
我知道泪水只是徒然，
你听不到也无法回应，
那么就让我为你致敬，
让心平静，把泪流干。
此刻你终于得以安息，
忘记所有的苦痛悲哀，
不必忧心当下和未来，
只是与家人欢乐相聚。
但我仍觉你人生短暂，
不相信你已弃世长眠。

♂ 摩西·奥沙罗

肯尼亚当代诗人。

No. 3

A Farewell

Harriet Monroe

Good—bye!—no, do not grieve that it is over,
 The perfect hour;
That the winged joy, sweet honey—loving rover,
 Flits from the flower.

Grieve not—it is the law. Love will be flying—
 Yes, love and all.
Glad was the living—blessed be the dying.
 Let the leaves fall.

No. 3

告别

哈丽特·门罗

再见！不，不要为结束而悲伤
这完美的时刻，
飞扬的快乐，游荡的采蜜者
自鲜花中掠过。

不要悲伤，这是定律。爱是会上浮。
是的，爱与其他什么。
活着的人是幸福，临终的人是有福。
就让绿叶凋落。

哈丽特·门罗

1860—1936，美国诗人、编辑，《诗刊》杂志创立者，知名作品有《我热爱我的生命》。

No. 4

A Farewell

Alfred Tennyson

Flow down, cold rivulet, to the sea,
Thy tribute wave deliver:
No more by thee my steps shall be,
For ever and for ever.

Flow, softly flow, by lawn and lea,
A rivulet then a river:

No. 4

告别

阿尔弗雷德·丁尼生

流向大海吧，清冽的小溪，
献上你层层的涟漪。
你身边不再有我的足迹，
永永远远，相会无期。

轻轻流淌吧，穿过草坪草地，
汇成河流：

Nowhere by thee my steps shall be
For ever and for ever.

But here will sigh thine alder tree
And here thine aspen shiver;
And here by thee will hum the bee,
For ever and for ever.

A thousand suns will stream on thee,
A thousand moons will quiver;
But not by thee my steps shall be,
For ever and for ever.

你身边不再有我的足迹，
永永远远，相会无期。

在这里，你的桤树会叹息
在这里，你的白杨会战栗
在这里，蜜蜂在你身边奔忙，
永永远远，相会无期。

一千轮太阳会洒落你身，
一千轮明月将摇落玉体；
你身边不再有我的足迹，
永永远远，相会无期。

阿尔弗雷德·丁尼生

1809—1892，英国维多利亚时代诗人，代表作品为组诗《悼念集》《国王叙事诗》等。

No. 5

Break, Break, Break

Alfred, Lord Tennyson

Break, break, break,
On thy cold grey stones, O Sea!
And I would that my tongue could utter
The thoughts that arise in me.

O well for the fisherman's boy,
That he shouts with his sister at play!
O well for the sailor lad,
That he sings in his boat on the bay!

No. 5

破碎，破碎，破碎

阿尔弗雷德·丁尼生

破碎，破碎，破碎
大海啊，破碎在灰冷的礁石
但愿我的言语能说出
我内心涌起的情思

多幸福啊，那渔家小伙儿
在和妹妹嬉戏、叫喊！
多幸福啊，那少年水手
唱着歌儿在海湾里划船！

And the stately ships go on
To their haven under the hill;
But O for the touch of a vanish'd hand,
And the sound of a voice that is still!

Break, break, break,
At the foot of thy crags, O Sea!
But the tender grace of a day that is dead,
Will never come back to me.

还有那些庄严的船舶
正驶归山下的港口，
但我只求再听到那已沉寂的声音，
再触碰那只已消逝的手！

破碎，破碎，破碎
大海啊，在岩石脚下破碎！
可温柔美好的日子已消逝，
一去再也难回。

No. 6

Remember

Christina Rossetti

Remember me when I am gone away,
Gone far away into the silent land;
When you can no more hold me by the hand,
Nor I half turn to go, yet turning stay.
Remember me when no more day by day
You tell me of our future that you plann'd:
Only remember me; you understand
It will be late to counsel then or pray.
Yet if you should forget me for a while
And afterwards remember, do not grieve:
For if the darkness and corruption leave
A vestige of the thoughts that once I had,
Better by far you should forget and smile
Than that you should remember and be sad.

No. 6

记

克里斯蒂娜·罗塞蒂

你要记住我，当我离去，
去向那遥远的寂静之地；
当你再也不能牵我的手，
而我再也不能欲留还拒。
记住我，当你再也不能
天天描述对未来的预期；
只要把我牢记，你明白
劝告或者祈求再已无益。
如果你暂时忘记我一阵
又重新想起，你莫悲戚。
如果黑暗和腐朽能留下
我曾经思考的些许痕迹，
那你最好笑着把我忘记
也不要悲伤地把我忆起。

克里斯蒂娜·罗塞蒂

1830—1894，英国19世纪诗人，主要作品集有《妖魔集市》《王子的历程》《赛会》等。

No. 7

The Last Night that She Lived

Emily Dickinson

The last Night that She lived
It was a Common Night
Except the Dying—this to Us
Made Nature different

We noticed smallest things—
Things overlooked before
By this great light upon our Minds
Italicized—as 'twere.

As We went out and in
Between Her final Room

No. 7

最后一夜

艾米莉·狄金森

她生前最后一夜
那一夜极为平常
于我们而言，使之不同的
只是死亡
我们注意到了最小的事——
而之前我们毫不在乎
在这伟大光辉闪过我们头脑时
仿佛变得——格外突出

我们来回穿梭于
她弥留的房间

And Rooms where Those to be alive
Tomorrow were, a Blame
That Others could exist
While She must finish quite
A Jealousy for Her arose
So nearly infinite—

We waited while She passed—
It was a narrow time—
Too jostled were Our Souls to speak
At length the notice came.
She mentioned, and forgot—
Then lightly as a Reed
Bent to the Water, struggled scarce—
Consented, and was dead—

And We—We placed the Hair—
And drew the Head erect—
And then an awful leisure was
Belief to regulate—

与其他明日尚存者的
房间，似乎是个责难
别人可以继续生存
而她必须离开世间
她生出的忌妒
几近无限——

我们等候着她过世——
时间并不多——
我们的灵魂拥挤得无法言语
直到最后的时刻。
她要说些什么，而后忘了——
像芦苇一样，轻轻地
弯向水边，没有挣扎——
默许一般地，离去——

而我们——我们规整下她的头发——
摆正她的头——
而后，需要好长时间
恢复生活的正常——

艾米莉·狄金森

1830—1886，美国传奇诗人，20世纪现代主义诗歌的先驱，代表作品有《云暗》《逃亡》《希望》《战场》《天使》《这是鸟儿们回来的日子》《神奇的书》等。

No. 8

A Dirge

Christina Rossetti

Why were you born when the snow was falling?
You should have come to the cuckoo's calling,
Or when grapes are green in the cluster,
Or, at least, when lithe swallows muster
For their far off flying
From summer dying.
Why did you die when the lambs were cropping?
You should have died at the apples' dropping,
When the grasshopper comes to trouble,
And the wheat—fields are sodden stubble,
And all winds go sighing
For sweet things dying.

No. 8

挽歌

克里斯蒂娜·罗塞蒂

为何你在白雪飘零时降生？
你的到来应迎着杜鹃的欢啼，
或是在串串葡萄青茂的时节，
或者，至少当那些成群的燕子
在长夏将尽时开始
漫长遥远地迁徙。
为何你在羔羊降生时离世？
你的逝去当随着苹果的纷纷坠地，
那时飞蝗遍野，
顷顷麦田满目疮痍，
所有的风儿都奔走哀叹
为这一切美好的凋敝。

No. 9

The Last Waltz

Boris Vian

Last diary

Last crescent

Dull morning

Of passers—by

And it is the end of the problem

Last sunshine

Last trump

Last coffee

Last sou

Goodbye，I'm leaving you

Last hotel

Last love

Last kiss

Last day

No. 9

最后的华尔兹

鲍里斯·维昂

最后的日记
最后的月牙
路上行人
无聊的早晨
这是问题的终结
最后的阳光
最后的王牌
最后的咖啡
最后一个苏
再见，我要离开你

最后的旅馆
最后的欢爱
最后的亲吻
最后的一天

Goodbye all the things I love

Last remorse

Last blues

Last decoration

Last evening

I'm leaving without a goodbye

Last waltz and no tomorrow

My heart will no longer feel pain

Last waltz for the scent of jasmine

And the quays of Seine

Last goodnight

A little for you

Last hope

Last of everything

Sleep， the night is so calm

Last pavement

Last cigarette

Last glance

Last jump

Nothing left but a large circle in the waters...

再见，我所爱的一切
最后的懊悔
最后的忧郁
最后的装饰
最后的黄昏

我走了，不说再见
最后的华尔兹　没有明天
我的心再感觉不到痛苦
最后的华尔兹　为了茉莉花香
为了塞纳河的码头

最后的晚安
只给你一点
最后的希望
最后的一切
睡吧，夜是如此宁静
最后的路面
最后的香烟
最后一瞥
最后一跃
只留下水中激起的涟漪

鲍里斯·维昂

1920—1959，法国小说家、剧作家、诗人。他在巴黎中央工艺美术学校时开始创作诗歌，写过电影剧本。代表作有《岁月的泡沫》《我唾弃你们的坟墓》《北京的秋天》《蚂蚁》等，戏剧作品有《创建帝国的人们》《全部屠宰》和《将军们的点心》，去世后发表诗集《我不愿死》。

No. 10

Song

Christina Rossetti

When I am dead, my dearest,
Sing no sad songs for me;
Plant thou no roses at my head,
Nor shady cypress tree;
Be the green grass above me
With showers and dewdrops wet;
And if thou wilt, remember,
And if thou wilt, forget.

No. 10

歌

克里斯蒂娜·罗塞蒂

如果我死了，亲爱的，
不要为我唱悲伤的歌曲；
坟畔无须蔷薇飘香，
也不用栽松柏翳翳；
做我冢上的青草吧，
长沐于露珠细雨；
要是你想，就常把我忆起，
要么就干脆，把我忘记。

I shall not see the shadows,
I shall not feel the rain;
I shall not hear the nightingale
Sing on, as if in pain;
And dreaming through the twilight
That doth not rise nor set,
Haply I may remember,
And haply may forget.

我再也看不到那翳翳的松柏，
也感受不到那缠绵的雨滴；
我再也听不到那夜莺
断肠泣血的悲啼；
在永恒的暮光中，
我，就此睡去，
或许，我会把你想起，
或者，我选择把你忘记。

No. 11

A Dream Within a Dream

Edgar Allanv Poe

Take this kiss upon the brow!
And, in parting from you now,
Thus much let me avow—
You are not wrong, who deem
That my days have been a dream;

Yet if hope has flown away
In a night, or in a day,
In a vision, or in none,
Is it therefore the less gone?

No. 11

梦中之梦

埃德加·爱伦·坡

受我眉间一吻！
在这别离时分，
我终究可以承认：
你曾说我人生空幻，
此言并未失真。

但若希望已鸿飞渺渺
于夜晚，抑或于白天，
于幻景，抑或于虚无，
是否就可有更多留存？

All that we see or seem
Is but a dream within a dream.
I stand amid the roar
Of a surf—tormented shore,
And I hold within my hand
Grains of the golden sand—
How few! yet how they creep
Through my fingers to the deep,
While I weep—while I weep!
O God! can I not grasp
Them with a tighter clasp?
O God! can I not save
One from the pitiless wave?
Is all that we see or seem
But a dream within a dream?

我们看见或似见的一切
不过就是一场梦中之梦。
我站在海边
倾听惊涛拍岸，
我将大把的金沙
努力地握在掌间——
那么一点！可它们
还是无情地从我指间滑落，
当我痛哭——两泪涟涟！
天啊！难道我
就不能再稍微握紧一点？
天啊！难道我就不能从
无情的浪涛中留下一粒？
难道我们看见或者似见的一切
仅是一场大梦？且在它梦之间？

埃德加·爱伦·坡

1809—1849，19世纪美国诗人、小说家和文学评论家，美国浪漫主义思潮时期的重要成员。其代表作品有小说《黑猫》《厄舍府的倒塌》，诗歌《乌鸦》《安娜贝尔·丽》等。

No. 12

Stanzas. —April, 1814

Percy Bysshe Shelley

Away! the moor is dark beneath the moon,
Rapid clouds have drunk the last pale beam of even:
Away! the gathering winds will call the darkness soon,
And profoundest midnight shroud the serene lights of heaven.

Pause not! the time is past! Every voice cries, 'Away!'
Tempt not with one last tear thy friend's ungentle mood:
Thy lover's eye, so glazed and cold, dares not entreat thy stay:
Duty and dereliction guide thee back to solitude.

Away, away! to thy sad and silent home;
Pour bitter tears on its desolated hearth;

No. 12

诗节——1814 年 4 月

珀西·比希·雪莱

去吧！月下的荒野是如此幽暗，
流云已吞没了黄昏最后的余晖。
去吧！晚风很快要把夜雾聚敛，
天空静谧的光彩要被午夜遮蔽。

别停！时光已逝！处处闻号哭：
去吧！莫洒别泪，免恋人伤悲。
她冰冷呆滞的眼不敢求你驻足，
职责和疏懒都令你向孤独回归。

去吧，去吧！去你幽寂的家园，
把痛苦的泪水洒入炉灰的凄凉，

Watch the dim shades as like ghosts they go and come,
And complicate strange webs of melancholy mirth.
The leaves of wasted autumn woods shall float around thine head,
The blooms of dewy Spring shall gleam beneath thy feet:
But thy soul or this world must fade in the frost that binds the dead,
Ere midnight's frown and morning's smile, ere thou and peace, may meet.

The cloud shadows of midnight possess their own repose,
For the weary winds are silent, or the moon is in the deep;
Some respite to its turbulence unresting ocean knows;
Whatever moves or toils or grieves hath its appointed sleep.

Thou in the grave shalt rest:—yet, till the phantoms flee,
Which that house and heath and garden made dear to thee erewhile,
Thy remembrance and repentance and deep musings are not free
From the music of two voices, and the light of one sweet smile.

看灰暗的影子来去似阴魂游散，
让忧郁和喜悦交织成奇怪的网。
你的头上会飘飞着残秋的落叶，
沾着露水的春天在你脚下绽放。
你的心或是人世在风霜中寂灭，
不等夜和晨光、你和恬静会面。

午夜阴暗的云影也会时常休憩，
风吹得倦了，或中天一轮明月。
狂暴不安的海洋总会停下瞬息，
运动、辛劳、苦悲，适时停歇。

你将在墓中安眠，但幻影婆娑，
让你沉迷于宅舍、荒野和亭园，
那记忆、悔恨和深思怎能摆脱
那甜美的一笑、奏乐般的交谈？

No. 13

Regret for the Departure of Friends

George Moses Horton

As smoke from a volcano soars in the air,
The soul of man discontent mounts from a sigh,
Exhaled as to heaven in mystical prayer,
Invoking that love which forbids him to die.

Sweet hope, lovely passion, my grief ever chase,
And scatter the gloom which veils pleasure's bright ray,
O lend me thy wings, and assist me to trace
The flight of my fair one when gone far away.

When the dim star of pleasure sets glimmering alone,
The planet of beauty on life's dreary shore,

No. 13

为朋友的离去感叹

乔治·摩西·霍顿

火山的烟尘在高空中弥漫，
人类的灵魂在沉重地叹息，
以神秘的祷词向天堂呼喊，
祈求爱神来临莫让他死去。

我的痛苦渴求希望与激情，
驱散那些遮蔽快乐的阴郁，
借我一双翅膀，让我追踪
已行远的爱人飞过的印记。

快乐的星星独自闪着微光，
阴沉的生活里凝结着美丽，

And th' fair bird of fancy forever is flown,
On pinions of haste to be heard of no more.
Hope, tell me, dear passion, thou wilt not forget,
To flourish still sweetly and blossom as gay,
Expelling like morning the gloom of regret,
When the lark of affection is gone far away.

If hurried into some unchangeable clime,
Where oceans of pleasure continually roll,
Far, far from the limited borders of time,
With a total division of body and soul.

Hope, tell me, dear passion, which must earth survive,
That love will be sweeter when nature is o'er,

幻想的青鸟已经永远飞逝，
驾着匆忙的翅膀无踪无际。
希望与激情知道你将依旧
甜美地盛开，愉快地绽放，
如晨曦驱散阴霾般的忧愁，
当情感已似云雀一样飞远。

若能匆忙进入不变的气候，
让愉悦的大海持续地翻滚，
远远避开时光有限的田畴，
将肉体和灵魂彻底地分离。

希望与激情知道地球存续，
当天地不在爱情更加甜美，

And still without pain though eternity live,
In the triumph of pleasure when time is no more.

O love, when the day—light of pleasure shall close,
Let the vesper of death break on life's dusky even;
Let the faint sun of time set in peace as it rose,
And eternity open thy morning in heaven.

Then hope, lovely passion, thy torch shall expire,
Effusing on nature life's last feeble ray;
While the night maid of love sets her taper on fire,
To guard smiling beauty from time far away.

全无苦痛，哪怕时光停止，
永恒存在的是愉悦的滋味。

爱人，当愉悦的光辉低垂，
就让死亡遮蔽生命的黄昏，
让太阳如升起般平静西坠，
永恒在天堂推开你的清晨。

希望与激情的光芒将熄灭，
向自然喷洒生命最后光彩；
而爱神的使女将点燃蜡烛，
护佑美丽免受时光的侵害。

乔治·摩西·霍顿

1798—1884，美国黑人诗人，做奴隶时就已经开始发表诗歌，代表作品有《自由的希望》《一个奴隶的诗》等。

No. 14

The Last Farewell

Marcus Garvey

Good—bye, my friend, in death we part,
To meet in realms more glorious:
A void I feel deep in my heart,
For much there was of love in us:

To see you go is awful pain,
For thou hast been a world to me;
But we shall meet for good again,
To see the light that hallows thee.

This death is only transient;
It leads to brighter and new vales,

No. 14

最后的告别

马库斯·加维

天人相隔怨重重，
唯盼天国再相逢。
我心空落无限恨，
此刻方觉情谊浓。

望君辞世痛欲狂，
宛如末日心惶惶。
只待天国长相聚，
凭栏把臂赏圣光。

死亡短暂且看轻，
转瞬光明又新生。

So wonderful, munificent,
As prophets tell in holy tales:

Go thou and wait for me a while,
And rest at God's fair borderland,
There with the angels you will smile,
In welcome to the saintly band.

Good—bye, my love, my truest friend;
All else in life for me to do
Was done ere I in grief attend
To say the last farewell to you:

The sod has covered you from view,
But memory dear shall finger still,
And I shall think in heart more true
Of all your good, and not of ill.

美妙丰饶何幸事，
先知圣言早点明。

君且暂去我即行，
天国边界可歇停。
携同天使齐带笑，
圣魂洁魄共相迎。

与君作别心怀悲，
身后诸事岂堪为？
离愁别恨长相扰，
此时只盼以身随。

一抔黄土掩君颜，
前尘往事却流连。
唯记恩情不记过，
我心深处忆更鲜。

马库斯·加维

1887—1940，黑人民族主义者，他宣扬黑人优越论，提倡非裔黑人返回非洲，协力创建一个统一的黑人国家。20世纪20年代早期，他拥有几百万的追随者。尽管他所发起的运动并没有取得持久的成效，但他的信条后来成为黑人反歧视斗争的驱动力。

On the Departure of the Nightingale 在夜莺离去之际 Tears, Idle Tears 泪水，无端的泪水 The Last Chrysanthemum 最后一朵菊花
The Wild Honey Suckle 野金银花 To Daffodils 咏水仙 Flowers, Dear Flowers, Farewell！永别了，美丽的花儿 Why Do Our Joys Depart? 为什么快乐总要离去？
The Last Rose of Summer 夏日最后一朵玫瑰 The Falling of the Leaves 叶落时分
On a Faded Violet 咏一朵枯萎的紫罗兰 Departure 离开 Farewell 告别 Farewell to Summer 与夏日为别 A Farewell 别辞
Farewell Frost, or Welcome Spring 道别冰霜，迎接春天 Farewell 别离辞

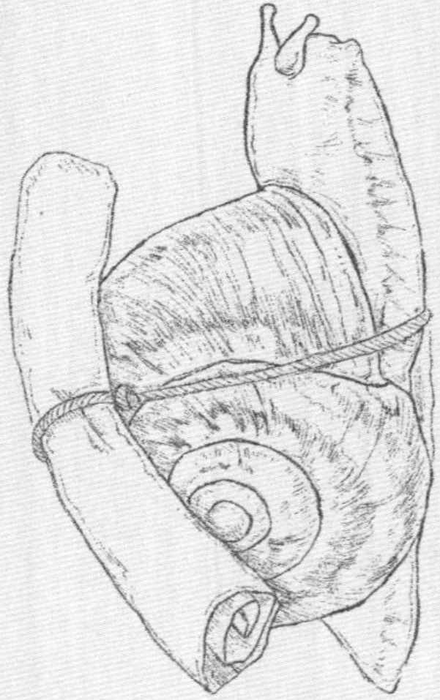

Moving by Sight

伤景

No. 1

On the Departure of the Nightingale

Charlotte Smith

Sweet poet of the woods, a long adieu!
Farewell soft minstrel of the early year!
Ah! 'twill be long ere thou shalt sing anew,
And pour thy music on the night's dull ear.
Whether on spring thy wandering flights await,
Or whether silent in our groves you dwell,
The pensive muse shall own thee for her mate,
And still protect the song she loves so well.
With cautious step the love—lorn youth shall glide
Through the lone brake that shades thy mossy nest;
And shepherd girls from eyes profane shall hide
The gentle bird who sings of pity best:
For still thy voice shall soft affections move,
And still be dear to sorrow and to love!

No. 1

在夜莺离去之际

夏洛特·史密斯

再见！森林中甜美的诗人，
再见！往日里柔情的歌手，
会很久听不到你放声欢唱，
让夜为你的歌声徒劳留守。
不论你是在春天等待盘旋，
还是在树林中静静地栖息，
忧郁的女神都会与你相伴，
护佑着她如此喜爱的乐辞。
相思的少年会小心地来此，
翻越过你布满青苔的孤巢；
为了避开俗世双眼的亵渎，
牧女会藏起吟唱温情的鸟：
你的声音仍打动甜美情感，
对悲伤抑或爱情珍贵依然！

夏洛特·史密斯

1749—1806，英国浪漫主义诗人和小说家，曾发起英语十四行诗复兴运动，参与创建哥特小说和感伤主义传统，其代表作品有诗集《悲歌十四行诗》，小说《古老庄园》等。

No. 2

Tears, Idle Tears

Alfred Tennyson

Tears, idle tears, I know not what they mean,
Tears from the depth of some divine despair
Rise in the heart, and gather to the eyes,
In looking on the happy Autumn—fields,
And thinking of the days that are no more.

Fresh as the first beam glittering on a sail,
That brings our friends up from the underworld,
Sad as the last which reddens over one
That sinks with all we love below the verge;

No. 2

泪水，无端的泪水

阿尔弗雷德·丁尼生

泪水，无端的泪水，我无从知其意，
它们来自绝望的深处
升腾于心，汇聚于目，
向欢乐的秋野眺望，
忆起那永不复返的时光。

清新，如第一缕微光在帆间闪烁，
让我们忆起逝去的友朋，
悲伤，如最后一缕残红
带着我们的爱沉入地平线；

So sad, so fresh,
the days that are no more.
Ah, sad and strange as in dark summer dawns
The earliest pipe of half-awaken'd birds
To dying ears, when unto dying eyes
The casement slowly grows a glimmering square;
So sad, so strange, the days that are no more.

Dear as remember'd kisses after death,
And sweet as those by hopeless fancy feign'd
On lips that are for others; deep as love,
Deep as first love, and wild with all regret;
O Death in Life, the days that are no more!

如此悲伤，如此清新，
那时光永不复返。
啊，悲伤又陌生，如夏日破晓前
初醒的鸟儿啾啾啼鸣
声声入耳，睁开眼睛
窗扉缓缓透出微亮；
如此悲伤，如此清新，那永不复返的时光。

珍贵如永生难忘之吻，
甜蜜似落在别人唇间
无望的遐想，深刻如爱恋，
如初恋，不顾一切地疯狂；
噢，生命中的死亡，那些永不复返的时光！

No. 3

The Last Chrysanthemum

Thomas Hardy

Why should this flower delay so long
To show its tremulous plumes?
Now is the time of plaintive robin—song,
When flowers are in their tombs.

Through the slow summer, when the sun
Called to each frond and whorl
That all he could for flowers was being done,
Why did it not uncurl?

It must have felt that fervid call
Although it took no heed,

No. 3

最后一朵菊花

托马斯·哈代

这朵花为何拖延如此之久
展示自己颤抖的花绒？
现在已是知更哀鸣的时刻，
花儿都已葬入了坟冢。

漫长的夏季里，太阳应邀
造访每片叶儿和花瓣，
他已为花朵倾尽所有，
为何这朵花还未展颜？

它一定感到了召唤的炽热，
但它却丝毫没有在意，

Waking but now, when leaves like corpses fall,
And saps all retrocede.
Too late its beauty, lonely thing,
The season's shine is spent,
Nothing remains for it but shivering
In tempests turbulent.

Had it a reason for delay,
Dreaming in witlessness
That for a bloom so delicately gay
Winter would stay its stress?

I talk as if the thing were born
With sense to work its mind;
Yet it is but one mask of many worn
By the Great Face behind.

此刻苏醒，树叶纷纷掉落，
汁液也都已复归大地 。
寂寞的花儿美丽绽放太迟，
季节已经消逝了荣光，
无物为它存留，只余战栗，
孤独地面对雨暴风狂。

难道它真有原因如此拖延，
抑或愚蠢地异想天开，
对于如此娇柔欢快的鲜妍，
严冬会变得温柔可爱？

瞧我说的，仿佛这东西
生来就有思考的能力；
然而，这不过是伟大上帝
佩戴的诸多面具之一。

托马斯·哈代

1840—1928，英国著名诗人、小说家，代表作品 有《德伯家的苔丝》《无名的裘德》《韦塞克斯诗集》等。

No. 4

The Wild Honey Suckle

Philip Freneau

Fair flower, that dost so comely grow,
Hid in this silent, dull retreat,
Untouched thy honeyed blossoms blow,
Unseen thy little branches greet;
No roving foot shall crush thee here,
No busy hand provoke a tear.

By Nature's self in white arrayed,
She bade thee shun the vulgar eye,
And planted here the guardian shade,
And sent soft waters murmuring by;

No. 4

野金银花

菲利普·弗瑞诺

美丽的花儿，你粲然绽放，
隐藏在这清幽寂静的地方，
未经染指的花蕊吐露芳馨，
无人垂顾的枝条随风摇荡；
游子不来侵你的玉体，
过客不曾催你的泪滴。

自然赐予你一袭素裹银装，
让你得以远离凡俗的目光，
她赐你一片葱葱绿荫环绕，
潺潺流淌的溪水常伴身旁；

Thus quietly thy summer goes,
Thy days declining to repose.
Smit with those charms, that must decay,
I grieve to see your future doom;
They died—nor were those flowers more gay,
The flowers that did in Eden bloom;
Unpitying frosts, and Autumn's power
Shall leave no vestige of this flower.

From morning suns and evening dews
At first thy little being came;
If nothing once, you nothing lose,
For when you die you are the same;
The space between, is but an hour,
The frail duration of flower.

恬静的夏日流逝倏然，
你终究难免红消香断。
妩媚动人却无法盛颜久长，
落花满地，令我黯然神伤；
纵然在伊甸园，百花齐放，
也难免一时凋零满目凄凉；
冷酷寒霜，无情西风
泯灭了你的一切踪影。

初晨的阳光与暮晚的露珠
孕育了你最初娇小的生命；
本无一物，你亦无物可失，
死后与生前并无太多不同；
生死旅程，仿佛瞬间，
花期易逝，生命苦短。

☙ 菲利普·弗瑞诺

1752—1832，美国独立革命时期著名诗人，美国革命战争后期最杰出的作家。代表作有诗歌《英国囚船》《野金银花》《印第安人墓地》等。

No. 5

To Daffodils

Robert Herrick

Fair Daffodils, we weep to see
You haste away so soon;
As yet the early-rising sun
Has not attain'd his noon.
Stay, stay,
Until the hasting day
Has run
But to the even-song;
And, having pray'd together, we
Will go with you along.

No. 5

咏水仙

罗伯特·赫里克

美丽的水仙花，我们垂泪
看你凋谢得如此匆忙；
仿佛初生的日头
尚未迎来正午的辉煌。
且住，且住，
待匆忙的太阳
开始
把暮歌唱响；
让我们共同祈祷，
相伴在离去的路上。

We have short time to stay, as you,
We have as short a spring;
As quick a growth to meet decay,
As you, or anything.
We die
As your hours do, and dry
Away,
Like to the summer's rain;
Or as the pearls of morning's dew,
Ne'er to be found again.

我们此生短暂，如你般，
我们的青春亦不久长；
如生长到凋零般迅速，
与你，与万物一样。
我们死去
像你的时光，
枯萎，
如夏日的雨，
又如清晨的露珠，
再也找不到痕迹。

ɞ 罗伯特·赫里克

1591—1674，英国资产阶级时期和复辟时期的“骑士派”诗人之一，代表作有《致水仙》《樱桃熟了》等。

No. 6

Flowers, Dear Flowers, Farewell!

Louisa May Alcott

'We are sending you, dear flowers,
Forth alone to die,
Where your gentle sisters may not weep
O'er the cold graves where you lie;
But you go to bring them fadeless life
In the bright homes where they dwell,
And you softly smile that 't is so,
As we sadly sing farewell.

No. 6

永别了，美丽的花儿！

路易莎·梅·阿尔考特

我们正在送你，亲爱的花儿
孤独地死去，
那里你温柔的姐妹或许不会哭泣
面对你冰冷的坟茔；
但你将给她们居住的光明的家园
带去永不褪色的生命，
对此你温婉地微笑，
我们伤心歌唱为你送行。

O plead with gentle words for us,
And whisper tenderly
Of generous love to that cold heart,
And it will answer ye;
And though you fade in a dreary home,
Yet loving hearts will tell
Of the joy and peace that you have given:
Flowers, dear flowers, farewell !

请许给我们温柔的言辞，
在耳边轻柔低语，
将慷慨的爱献给那颗冰冷的心，
让它对你做出期许；
纵然你在那可怕的居所中逝去，
满怀爱意的心儿也会记下，
记下你曾经奉献的快乐和安宁：
永别了，花儿，我亲爱的花！

路易莎·梅·阿尔考特

1832—1888，美国小说家和诗人，
代表作有小说《小妇人》。

No. 7

Why Do Our Joys Depart?

Walter Landor

Why do our joys depart
For cares to seize our heart?
I know not. Nature says
Obey; and Man obeys.
I see, and know not why,
Thorns live and roses die.

No. 7

为什么快乐总要离去？

沃尔特·兰德尔 ❧

为什么快乐总要离去
留下忧愁把我们心灵折磨？
我不知。自然只是说
听话，而我们也就只能听着。
我见到了，但就是不明白，
为什么荆棘得存而玫瑰花落。

❧ 沃尔特·兰德尔

1775—1864，英国作家和诗人，著名作品有散文《想象的对话》和诗歌《罗丝·埃尔默》等。

No. 8

The Last Rose of Summer

Thomas Moore

`Tis the last rose of summer
Left blooming alone;
All her lovely companions
Are faded and gone;
No flower of her kindred,
No rosebud is nigh,
To reflect back her blushes,
To give sigh for sigh.

No. 8

夏日最后一朵玫瑰

托马斯·穆尔

夏日最后一朵玫瑰
独自绽放幽香；
其他可爱的伴侣
都已开败消亡；
附近没有同类的
花朵抑或花蕾
来映照她的羞颜，
来回应她的忧伤。

I`ll not leave thee, thou lone one!
To pine on the stem;
Since the lovely are sleeping,
Go, sleep thou with them.
Thus kindly I scatter
Thy leaves o`er the bed,
Where thy mates of the garden
Lie scentless and dead.

So soon may I follow,
When friendships decay,
And from Love`s shining circle
The gems drop away.
When true hearts lie withered
And fond ones are flown,
Oh! who would inhabit
This bleak world alone?

我不会抛下你，孤独的花儿！
任你在枝上憔悴了容颜，
既然诸多美丽都已沉睡，
去吧，与它们同眠。
我温柔地用你的叶子
将你的温床撒满，
在那里你园中的伴侣
也早已蕊落香残。

友情一旦逝去，
我也会很快作别，
爱情的闪闪光环中
珍奇已经幻灭。
爱人一旦离飞，
真心一旦凋谢，
啊，谁还会独自徘徊
在这荒凉世界？

托马斯·穆尔

1779—1852，爱尔兰诗人和歌手，代表作有诗歌《吟游男孩》和《夏日最后一朵玫瑰》等。

No. 9

The Falling of the Leaves

William Butler Yeats

Autumn is over the long leaves that love us,
And over the mice in the barley sheaves;
Yellow the leaves of the rowan above us,
And yellow the wet wild—strawberry leaves.
The hour of the waning of love has beset us,
And weary and worn are our sad souls now;
Let us part, ere the season of passion forget us,
With a kiss and a tear on thy drooping brow.

No. 9

叶落时分

威廉·巴特勒·叶芝 ☙

秋色侵染了庇佑我们的长叶，
那麦堆中的田鼠也被催变老；
我们头顶的花楸叶已经变黄，
野草莓湿漉的叶子也已枯槁。
激情不断地衰退让我们困扰，
悲伤的灵魂已变得倦乏疲劳；
让我们分手吧，趁余情尚在，
带着眼泪，吻你低垂的眉梢。

☙ 威廉·巴特勒·叶芝

1865—1939，爱尔兰诗人、剧作家和散文家，著名的神秘主义者，“爱尔兰文艺复兴运动”的领袖，1923年获诺贝尔文学奖，代表诗歌有《钟楼》《盘旋的楼梯》等。

No. 10

On a Faded Violet

Percy Bysshe Shelley

The odor from the flower is gone
Which like thy kisses breathed on me;
The color from the flower is flown
Which glowed of thee and only thee!
A shrivelled, lifeless, vacant form,
It lies on my abandoned breast;
And mocks the heart, which yet is warm,
With cold and silent rest.
I weep — my tears revive it not;
I sigh — it breathes no more on me:
Its mute and uncomplaining lot
Is such as mine should be.

No. 10

咏一朵枯萎的紫罗兰

珀西·比希·雪莱

这一朵花已经失去了香味，
就像你的吻，曾对我呼吸；
那鲜艳的颜色也已经消退，
不再闪耀着你，唯一的你！
一个枯萎僵硬死亡的躯体，
茫然停留在我凄凉的前胸，
它以冷漠还有沉默的安息
嘲笑着这依旧温暖的心灵。
我哭，泪水不能让它重生！
我叹，它不能再向我吐息！
这沉默而无怨无悔的宿命
虽是它的，对我却也适宜。

No. 11

Departure

J. Corson Miller

His blind hands groped
For smooth egress
Along the dear familiar gate,
In mute caress.

And, looking down
Musingly a bit,
He saw the spot where, as a child,
He used to sit.

No. 11

离开

J. 科尔森·米勒

他的手抚摸着，
带着无声的温存，
那平滑的出口，
那亲切熟悉的大门。

低下头，
沉思些许时间，
他看到了，
那个儿时常坐的地点。

He studied the ancient house
With its gabled pride,
Remembering the wind that worried the curtain
Where his mother died.

And he thought of the day
That love died too,
When he found his young and wayward wife
Untrue

Somewhere from the sleep-veiled river,
Like a madman's cry,
A lone loon flung him finally
Goodbye.

他凝望着那山墙高耸
古老的房子，
忆起风轻拂着窗帘，
他的母亲在那里长逝。

他也想起了那一天，
他的爱情亦逝，
当他发现他年轻任性的妻子，
不再忠实。

自某处朦胧的溪流，
传来疯狂的哭喊。
那是一个孤独的潜鸟跟他说
再见。

J. 科尔森·米勒

美国诗人，虔诚的天主教徒，生卒年不详。

No. 12

Farewell

Thomas E. Spencer（1845—1911）

As we travel Life's weary journey,
And plod through the gathering years,
With our burdens of care and sorrow,
O'er a pathway bedewed with tears.
If, perchance, for a fleeting moment
Our hearts should with rapture swell,
We have added but one more sorrow,
When we bid the glad time "Farewell".

I have watched the bright dawn awaking,
And noted each changing light,

No. 12

告别

托马斯·E. 斯宾塞

当踏上人生疲惫的旅程，
艰难地走过累积的年岁，
背负我们的忧虑和悲伤，
在这一路上洒满了泪水。
如果，或许，只是一瞬
我们的心能够充满狂喜，
那不过是徒增一次伤悲，
因我们终会向快乐告辞。

我看着明亮的黎明醒来，
看到每一丝变幻的光彩，

As the sun, in its morning splendour,
Dispelled the dark gloom of night.
I have welcomed its bright rays stealing
Over hill—top, and wood, and dell;
Yet, my joy was alloyed with sorrow,
As I bade the bright stars "Farewell".

I have seen the red sun descending
To its home in the glowing west,
Whilst the tremulous voice of nature
Was solemnly lulled to rest.
I have welcomed the stars, appearing,
And greeted them one by one,
Yet, my greeting was toned with sadness,
As I said "Farewell" to the sun.

When we welcome the summer sunshine,
Farewell to the flowers of Spring.
Adieu to the fruits of Autumn,
When we welcome the frosty king.

太阳在每日清晨的辉煌，
驱走了夜色黑暗的阴霾。
我曾欢迎它的明光播洒
在那树林、山谷和山顶；
但我的喜悦与悲伤共存，
当我作别那明亮的星星。

我曾亲眼看到红日下坠
西归于它那闪亮的家园，
自然中种种颤抖的声音
也静穆地陷入安息睡眠。
我也曾欢迎繁星的出现，
并逐一向它们问候致意，
但我的问候总伴着悲伤，
因为那时我正告别阳光。

当我们欢迎夏日的阳光，
我们却是在向春花作别。
那是向累累秋实说再见，
当我们把冬日严寒迎接。

Good—bye to the joys of childhood,
When vigorous youth appears;
Then—a season of strife and turmoil,
And—farewell to the vanished years.

I am sighing a farewell message,
As I sit in the gathering gloom.
Farewell to all earthly sorrows,
Then—rest, in the silent tomb.
Farewell to the trees, and flowers,
To mountain, and stream, and dell,
Farewell to the glorious sunlight,
To the moon and stars, "Farewell"

当青春的活力蓬勃而出，
那童年的快乐就会消失；
然后是冲突混乱的季节，
最终又告别逝去的时日。

我陷于越积越厚的忧郁，
以悲叹传送离别的信息。
告别人世间所有的忧伤，
然后长眠在静寂的墓里。
告别树木，告别花和草，
告别幽谷、溪流和高山，
告别那光辉灿烂的阳光，
告别月和繁星，“再见”。

托马斯·E. 斯宾塞
澳大利亚作家，著名作品有诗集《麦克杜格尔如何得高分》。

No. 13

Farewell to Summer

George Arnold

SUMMER is fading; the broad leaves that grew
So freshly green, when June was young, are falling;
And, all the whisper—haunted forest through,
The restless birds in saddened tones are calling,
From rustling hazel copse and tangled dell,
"Farewell, sweet Summer,
Fragrant, fruity Summer,
Sweet, farewell!"

Upon the windy hills, in many a field,
The honey—bees hum slow, above the clover,

No. 13

与夏日为别

乔治·阿诺德

夏日将尽；六月初时
鲜绿的叶子，此刻纷纷坠下；
不安的鸟儿悲伤地鸣啼
催树丛瑟瑟，促幽谷纷杂，
沙沙低语萦绕在林间：
“再见了，甜美的夏日，
芳香的，丰硕的夏日，
亲爱的，再见！”

在风吹过的山间，在田野里，
蜜蜂在三叶草上辛勤地忙碌

Gleaning the latest sweets its blooms may yield,
And, knowing that their harvest—time is over,
Sing, half a lullaby and half a knell,
"Farewell, sweet Summer,
Honey—laden Summer,
Sweet, farewell!"

The little brook that babbles mid the ferns,
O'er twisted roots and sandy shallows playing,
Seems fain to linger in its eddied turns,
And with a plaintive, purling voice is saying
(Sadder and sweeter than my song can tell,
"Farewell, sweet Summer,
Warm and dreamy Summer,
Sweet, farewell!"

The fitful breeze sweeps down the winding lane
With gold and crimson leaves before it flying;
Its gusty laughter has no sound of pain,
But in the lulls it sinks to gentle sighing,

采摘着花儿刚产出的花蜜，
知道收获的季节行将结束，
它们唱着，半是悲伤，半是欣欢，
“再见了，甜美的夏日，
满是蜜露的夏日，
亲爱的，再见！”

蕨叶间流淌的溪水潺潺，
在弯曲的根茎和沙滩间嬉戏，
欢快地在旋涡中翻转，
用悲伤婉转的声音言语：
（我的歌描述不出这悲伤和甘甜）
“再见了，甜美的夏日，
温暖、轻柔的夏日，
亲爱的，再见！”

一阵阵微风吹过蜿蜒的小径，
红黄的叶子在风中飞舞；
迸发的笑声听不到任何悲声，
间歇里却把温柔的叹息倾吐，

And mourns the Summer's early broken spell,—
"Farewell, sweet Summer,
Rosy, blooming Summer,
Sweet, farewell!"

So bird and bee and brook and breeze make moan,
With melancholy song their loss complaining.
I too must join them, as I walk alone
Among the sights and sounds of Summer's waning...
I too have loved the season passing well...
So, farewell, Summer,
Fair but faded Summer,
Sweet, farewell!

摧毁夏日的咒语在哀叹：
“再见，甜美的夏日，
繁花绽放的夏日，
亲爱的，再见！”

鸟儿、蜜蜂、小溪和微风
都用忧郁的歌儿哀叹着失望
我也会加入它们，因我踽踽独行
面对着夏日将尽的声音与景象……
这将逝的季节也曾令我眷恋……
那么，再见，夏日，
美丽但凋零的夏日，
亲爱的，再见！

乔治·阿诺德

美国作家和诗人，代表作有《快乐的老教育家》。

No. 14

A Farewell

Amy Levy

The sad rain falls from Heaven,
A sad bird pipes and sings ;
I am sitting here at my window
And watching the spires of "King's."

O fairest of all fair places,
Sweetest of all sweet towns!
With the birds, and the greyness and greenness,
And the men in caps and gowns.

No. 14

别辞

艾米·里维

苦雨天际落
悲鸟吟离歌
窗前独静坐
举目望高阁

千城唯此美
万镇独此亲
颜色着群鸟
衣冠遮众人

All they that dwell within thee,
To leave are ever loth,
For one man gets friends, and another
Gets honour, and one gets both.

The sad rain falls from Heaven;
My heart is great with woe—
I have neither a friend nor honour,
Yet I am sorry to go.

诸君栖此地
安乐不忍去
有伴多嘉友
随身皆美誉

苦雨天际落
余心感悲戚
无誉少嘉友
何故不忍离?

☙ 艾米·里维

英国诗人、小说家和散文家，主要作品有小说《店铺传奇》和诗集《宗教和婚姻的歌谣》等。

No. 15

Farewell Frost, or Welcome Spring

Robert Herrick

Fled are the frosts, and now the fields appear
Reclothed in fresh and verdant diaper;
Thaw'd are the snows; and now the lusty Spring
Gives to each mead a neat enamelling;
The palms put forth their gems, and every tree
Now swaggers in her leafy gallantry.
The while the Daulian minstrel sweetly sings
With warbling notes her Terean sufferings.
—What gentle winds perspire! as if here

No. 15

道别冰霜，迎接春天

罗伯特·赫里克

寒霜已去，大地重新披上
那袭鲜艳嫩绿的衣裳；
冰雪消融，阳春生机勃勃
赐每片草地明丽颜色；
棕榈摇曳着手掌，每棵树
都炫耀着枝叶的丰足。
多尔的诗人用柔和的音符
甜美地吟唱她的痛苦。
风儿吹得多么温柔，好像

Never had been the northern plunderer
To strip the trees and fields, to their distress,
Leaving them to a pitied nakedness.
And look how when a frantic storm doth tear
A stubborn oak or holm, long growing there,—
But lull'd to calmness, then succeeds a breeze
That scarcely stirs the nodding leaves of trees;
So when this war, which tempest—like doth spoil
Our salt, our corn, our honey, wine, and oil,
Falls to a temper, and doth mildly cast
His inconsiderate frenzy off, at last,
The gentle dove may, when these turmoils cease,
Bring in her bill, once more, the branch of Peace.

北地肆虐未发生一样，
好像绿树碧野都从未褪色
只留下光秃秃的躯壳。
看疯狂的风暴曾如何撕裂
倔强的橡树抑或麻栎，
但那肆虐之后平和的清风
低垂的树叶都未扰动；
这战争，曾经像暴风一般
摧毁我们的柴米油盐，
此刻终于走向停歇，他那
无情的疯狂也已抛下。
当骚乱平息，温柔的鸽子
再次衔来和平的树枝。

罗伯特·赫里克

1591—1674，英国资产阶级时期和复辟时期的“骑士派”诗人之一。代表作品有《樱桃熟了》《致妙龄少女：莫负青春》《致水仙》等。

No. 16

Farewell

John Clare

Farewell to the bushy clump close to the river
And the flags where the butter-bump hides in forever;
Farewell to the weedy nook, hemmed in by waters;
Farewell to the miller's brook and his three bonny daughters;
Farewell to them all while in prison I lie—
In the prison a thrall sees naught but the sky.

Shut out are the green fields and birds in the bushes;
In the prison yard nothing builds,
blackbirds or thrushes.

No. 16

别离辞

约翰·克莱尔

再见了，河边茂密的灌木；
再见了，麻鸦栖居的菖蒲；
再见了，碧水环绕的草地；
再见了，磨工的溪水和他三个漂亮的女儿；
再见了，所有一切，而我躺在牢狱之中
狱中的奴隶，什么都看不见，除了天空。

遮蔽了林中的鸟儿和绿地
牢中一无所有，
也没有乌鸦和画眉。

Farewell to the old mill and dash of waters,
To the miller and, dearer still, to his three bonny daughters.
In the nook, the larger burdock grows near the green willow;
In the flood, round the moor-cock dashes under the billow;
To the old mill farewell, to the lock, pens, and waters,
To the miller himself, and his three bonny daughters.

再见了，古老的磨坊和流水，
再见了，磨工和他三个漂亮的女儿。
绿柳下，牛蒡在角落里生长；
旷野中，野鸡在松涛下飞奔；
再见了，古老的磨坊，那水闸、围栏和溪水，
再见了，磨工和他三个漂亮的女儿。

约翰·克莱尔

1793—1864，英国19世纪浪漫主义时期诗人，诗歌创作侧重于对自然的描写，以植物、动物、家乡以及爱情等主题见长，代表作品有诗集《乡村生活和自然景色的描写》等。

图书在版编目（CIP）数据

我们还会再见吗：汉、英 / 苗勇刚，贾宇萍编译. -- 北京：现代出版社，2019.6
ISBN 978-7-5143-7812-2

Ⅰ. ①我… Ⅱ. ①苗… ②贾… Ⅲ. ①诗集 – 世界 – 汉、英 Ⅳ. ①I12

中国版本图书馆CIP数据核字(2019)第100590号

我们还会再见吗

作　　者：苗勇刚　贾宇萍
责任编辑：申　晶
出版发行：现代出版社
地　　址：北京市安定门外安华里504号
邮政编码：100011
电　　话：010-64267325　64245264（兼传真）
网　　址：www.1980xd.com
电子邮箱：xiandai@cnpitc.com.cn
印　　刷：北京瑞禾彩色印刷有限公司

开　　本：880mm×1230mm　1/32　印　　张：6.25　字　　数：190千字
版　　次：2019年6月第1版　印　　次：2019年6月第1次印刷
书　　号：ISBN 978-7-5143-7812-2
定　　价：59.80元